SPOOKY OHIO:
13 TRADITIONAL TALES

Selected and retold by
Chris Woodyard

Illustrated by
Jessica Wiesel

**Kestrel
Publications**

1811 Stonewood Drive
Beavercreek, OH 45432

ALSO BY CHRIS WOODYARD

Haunted Ohio III: Still More Ghostly Tales from the Buckeye State
Haunted Ohio II: More Ghostly Tales from the Buckeye State
Haunted Ohio: Ghostly Tales from the Buckeye State
The Wright Stuff: A Guide to Life in the Dayton Area

See the last page of the book for how to order your own copy of
this book or these other books by Chris Woodyard

First Edition 1995
Typesetting: Copy Plus, Dayton, OH
Printed by C.J. Krehbiel, Cincinnati, OH
Library of Congress Catalog Card Number 91-75343

Woodyard, Chris
Spooky Ohio: 13 Traditional Tales/Chris Woodyard/Jessica Wiesel
SUMMARY: Traditional ghostlore collected from oral histories and
family traditions around Ohio.

ISBN: 0-9628472-3-2
1. Ghost Stories—United States—Ohio
2. Ghosts—United States—Ohio
3. Folklore—United States—Ohio
I. Woodyard, Chris II. Wiesel, Jessica III. Title
398.25 W912H
070.593 Wo
Z1033.L73

For my daughter, not-so-little-anymore green ghost
and favorite literary critic.

– C. W. –

For my Dad

– J. W. –

TABLE OF CONTENTS

INTRODUCTION

"I do believe in spooks, I do, I do, I do..."
—The Cowardly Lion, *The Wizard of Oz*—

D o *you* believe in spooks? The people who told these stories did. To them, ghosts were as real as the trees in the forest. And as scary as the wild animals that lurked behind every one of those trees.

These stories are called "folklore"—they are stories that *may* have really happened somewhere, sometime, but they have been told and retold and handed down until nobody really knows where they came from.

I found these stories in many different places: in libraries, in old books, in newspapers, from readers who sent me letters. At the back of the book I've told a little bit about the people who told them and where in Ohio they were found.

We all like being scared—especially when we're sitting in a cozy chair, in a room where the lights are bright. I think reading scary stories helps us deal with the real scary things in our lives. Scary stories are a *safe* way to scare ourselves—like riding the roller coaster at the park—we all *know* that it isn't going to come off the track (or is it?) but we still scream and cover our eyes.... When there isn't any real danger, it's fun to be scared!

So now—if you dare—make sure you have a flashlight, put your back to the wall or the blankets over your head, read 'em and creep....

A NOTE FOR
PARENTS AND TEACHERS

In a world full of real-life horrors, ghost stories are a constant favorite. When children are exposed to so much violence in video games, movies, and TV, why should they read scary stories?

1. Ghost stories draw in the most reluctant readers. Librarians constantly tell me that they can't keep ghost stories on the shelves. Roberta Simpson Brown, story-teller, teacher, and "The Queen of the Cold-Blooded Tales," says that spooky tales get her students' attention better than anything else she's tried.

2. Ghost stories often help children confront and conquer their fears. The world can be a frightening place, but the "delicious shivers" generated by a spooky story are very different from the scary *real* violence on the evening news. And a ghost tale may provide a safe framework for working out those real fears. As a child, I constantly terrified myself with ghost stories, yet there was something exhilarating in finding myself still alive the next morning! It is important for a child to realize that he can be frightened and still survive.

3. Ghost stories are a way to scare ourselves silly—safely—like riding the roller-coaster at the amusement park. Most ghost stories, particularly the traditional ones, follow predictable paths. This is comforting to the reader.

4. These traditional stories can be a window onto a different world—the world of the past—where people wear different clothes, eat different foods, use different

words. And yet it is a world where some things—fear and greed, love and longing—never change. For some children, this may be their only way to connect with history.

5. Ghost stories may even probe the eternal mysteries of life and death and, for older children, suggest some important questions for discussion.

6. Most importantly—ghost stories are just plain fun!

So unplug the TV, turn out the lights, and prepare for a trip to that state of terror—*Spooky Ohio.*

THE BRIDE AT THE BRIDGE

On the morning of August 12, 1837, Esther Hale hummed happily to herself as she put on her white dress and veil. It was her wedding day. The table in the parlor was decorated with flowers and vines. The cake was in the kitchen, covered in cheesecloth to keep off the flies. The wedding was set for ten in the morning.

But by half past ten the groom had not arrived and the guests and the parson were beginning to fidget. At half past twelve, they climbed into their wagons and drove away. The messenger Esther sent could find no trace of her bridegroom. His cabin was deserted, said the man, and the ashes in the stove were cold.

When Esther's friends tried to help her to bed, Esther shook her head, the tears running down her face. Finally they left her sitting alone in the dark by the window of the parlor. When they returned the next morning, the curtains had been drawn, as if for a funeral. They were never again opened in Esther Hale's lifetime.

All summer Esther moved like a ghost through the house. In the kitchen, beetles tunneled through the cake. The wedding flowers withered under the spiders' veils in the parlor. Esther's friends coaxed her to eat and drink a little, but when they tried to get her to change her dress or remove the wedding decorations, she flew at them with claw-like fingers. Finally they left her alone.

Broken hearts kill slowly. Four months later a neighbor noticed that the door to Esther's house was open, banging back and forth in the December wind. He told the sheriff and the doctor who took a party of men to the dark house. Snow had drifted throughout the rooms like a white shroud.

Esther was slumped over the parlor window sill, her veil over her face. Someone held up a lantern. The doctor drew back the shredded lace. Esther had been dead for several weeks. When they saw the horror beneath, they silently covered her over again. She was buried so, shrouded in her wedding clothes.

But burial did not put an end to Esther Hale. It is said by the locals that you can still see her, dressed in white, looking for her bridegroom on the bridge over Beaver Creek in Columbiana County. She waits there every year on August 12, a hideous figure in tattered white satin and lace. And if she touches you, she will become young and beautiful again—but you will die.

So if you are in the area in early August, drive through quickly with your windows rolled up. And keep a sharp lookout for a skeletal woman in a wedding dress stained by the grave. For she will lunge at your car, her bony fingers scrabbling at your windows, desperate as Death to touch and claim your living flesh for her own.

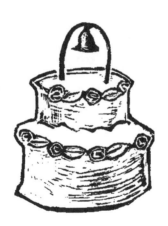

THE SEVEN DACHSHUNDS

One night an old stranger with a German accent came to the door of Dave Dye's big brick house which stood on Fairfield Pike near the edge of Yellow Springs in Greene County. He said he'd come all the way from Germany, and he was very tired.

"Well, that's pretty far to come in one day," said Dave, and invited the man, who wouldn't give his name, to stay the night. They sat up and roasted sausages and drank beer and swapped lies until about midnight when the old German began to get edgy.

"Have you good locks to your doors?" he asked finally.

"Best they make in Cincinnati," replied his host. "You're not worried about robbers are you?"

"Not robbers," said the old man. "Dogs."

"Dogs?" asked Dave, "What kind of dogs?"

The old man looked around him. "Dachshunds," he whispered.

Dave threw back his head and laughed until he caught the look of terror on the man's face. "Here now," he said soberly, "what's wrong?"

The old man buried his face in his hands. "In Germany I killed a man. He had wronged my daughter, but I had no choice but to flee on the first boat. Somehow the dead man's dogs followed me. They got on that boat and they have followed me ever since—all seven of them!"

Dave choked back another snort of laughter. The old man stood up, trembling.

"Open the door!" he ordered. Dave did so.

A little ways down the road Dave could hear a pack of dogs yapping, getting closer and closer. They weren't any dogs he knew.

"Now shut it!" said the German. Dave did so and sank back into his seat. Howling, the dogs swept down the road to the house. The men held their breath as they heard claws clicking on the porch, noses snuffling eagerly under the door, and then, a sudden, awful silence.

After a while the German stood up. "Tonight," he said, "I will fool them. You just wait and see." And he went off to bed.

Dave lay awake most of the night, thinking that every noise he heard was the dogs trying to break in. Bleary-eyed he knocked on the old man's door the next morning.

But the old man was gone, leaving the window open behind him.

Leaning out the window, Dave saw where the German had climbed down the trumpet vine to the grape arbor, where he had crawled along the arbor to the crabapple tree. In the dusty road he saw the marks of wagon wheels. The old man must have leaped from the tree into a passing wagon, away from the awful snuffling noses of the hell-hounds.

Dave got to know those hounds very well. For the next six nights the dogs yapped and howled around his house. And then they vanished as quietly as the German. Dave shivered as he wondered how they'd picked up the trail.

THE HEADLESS SOLDIER

In a rundown frame house near Fairfield in Greene County lived a family named Batdorf. After their son Charles was killed in the Civil War, they moved away and the house was rented by a family named Cox.

But the Coxes rarely lived in the house. They were always going "visiting" and it was whispered that they were afraid that the ghost of Charles Batdorf would return to the house—headless after his meeting with a shell at the Battle of the Wilderness.

While the Coxes went visiting, the neighborly Shaws kept an eye on the house.

One night in summer, Peggy Shaw and her mother went over to the old house to see that everything was all right. It was a moonlit night and Peggy could see the glittering pebbles on the path as clear as day.

"I heard someone walking down the gravel path to the house the night before last," said Mrs. Shaw, "I wonder if the Coxes have come back?"

When she and her daughter checked the house, they found it dark and empty. Feeling a little uneasy in spite of the moon, Peggy and her mother turned and headed back up the path.

Suddenly Mrs. Shaw stopped. Peggy felt her mother squeeze her hand and heard her whisper, "Who is that?"

Peggy looked but couldn't see anyone. There were some lilac bushes ahead, shining like silver in the moonlight. All at once Peggy saw someone step out from the bushes and start walking in their direction.

She heard the crunch of boots on gravel, saw the glint of moonlight on a button, heard the jingle of a pair of spurs. The figure was a hundred feet away when he stopped. For what seemed like ages, Peggy and her mother stood facing him. He was a young man in a white shirt and a blue uniform trimmed with two rows of brass buttons. And they saw that he had no head!

Frozen, they watched the figure move uncertainly in the moonlight, turning his neck stump this way and that. He's searching, Peggy thought. He can't find his way home... A scream bubbled up in her throat.

At the sound, the headless man stiffened, then began to shuffle towards them, his hands pawing the air. Mrs. Shaw pulled Peggy's arm. They ran all the way home as if a whole troop of headless cavalry was chasing them.

Once inside their well-lit kitchen, they looked at each other, breathless and white-faced, listening for footsteps outside.

"That was Charlie Batdorf," said Peggy's mother.

POKE-BONNET KATE

Back in the hills of Ross County was a village called Kidder's Creek. It was hardly a village—just a dirt road and a few houses and a store. On a nearby farm lived the Holtzmeiers—Joseph and Kate. They had two children, Carl and Jenny. Jenny was a beauty and she could have had her pick of the local boys, but her mama wouldn't let any boy even cross the front porch to come calling.

The minute Kate saw a boy coming up the path, she'd be out on the porch with her broom, her reddish-brown eyes burning at the intruder from the depths of the calico bonnet that surrounded her thin face. Then Kate would watch the boy slink away

and shake her fist if he didn't move fast enough.
After a while, most of the boys quit trying.

One of those local boys who pined for Jenny
Holtzmeier was named Ezra.He moved away and
found a wife and settled in Chillicothe, but all the
time—in the back of his mind—was the thought of
that pretty Jenny Holtzmeier, wasting away her youth
and beauty on that lonely farm.

Ezra's brother Sam still lived in Kidder's Creek
and one day Ezra told his wife Nellie that he wanted
to go visit his brother and family back home. It was
all right with her. Nellie didn't know Ezra's kinfolk
and didn't much care, so he went without her.

Sam made Ezra feel right at home. After supper,
by the fire, Ezra asked about all the neighboring
families, leading up to the Holtzmeiers.

Sam shook his head.

"Carl and the old man died a few years back
from overwork. The old lady, she lingered a little
and then passed on—from sheer meanness, I
reckon," said Sam. "They buried her in the front
yard of the house; she was too cheap to buy a place
in the churchyard."

"And Jenny?"

"Jenny sold most of the land. Now she lives all
by herself in the old house. Don't know what she
does all day."

"Since I'm in the area, I guess I ought to pay a
call," Ezra said casually. He and Sam joked at this
being the first time he'd be allowed on the porch.

And even though it was getting dark, he set out for the Holtzmeier's farm. He shivered as he climbed the stairs and crossed the porch, then laughed at himself.

Jenny, dressed in black, opened the door. She seemed pleased to see company although she didn't remember Ezra right off—that took him down a peg!—but she gave him tea and cake in the parlor. They talked about the old school days until the fire burned down. Ezra showed her a picture of his wife and kids.

"They look just like you," Jenny said sadly, and Ezra got the idea she wished she was married, with kids of her own.

Jenny was worn to a thread, her hands all rough and red, her hair going grey, and a scared look in her eye. Ezra didn't let on how disappointed he was. He still remembered the pretty girl he'd hankered for.

It was going on midnight before Ezra said his goodbyes and thanked Jenny kindly for her hospitality. She invited him to call anytime and Ezra, looking back at her stooped figure standing in the doorway, waved. Then he set off at a good pace, wanting to be off that spooky road. Suddenly he saw a flash of light beyond the trees to the right. He stopped and looked hard, then started walking again. Everything was dark and as still as those woods ever got.

Ezra went on a little way, supposing his eyes were playing tricks, when he saw another flash of light. This time he picked up a few good-sized stones and called, "Come out of those trees and face me."

He started towards the woods, and then he saw it. He couldn't quite make out what it was—it was grey and hunched over and didn't move. He threw one rock. The thing raised its arms. His stomach turned over, but he walked closer and threw another rock.

The thing started towards him and he realized what it was—a woman in a shawl and a deep poke-bonnet. It was Kate, her clothes and face all covered with grey grave mold. She didn't say a word, only silently shook her fist at him—just like she used to when he was a boy come to call on Jenny. And Ezra took off running, and never stopped till he reached his brother Sam's place.

THE BUGGY BOGLE

Enos Kay was a popular young man around Egypt Pike. He was a good student, went faithfully to church, and worked hard for his folks. And, like most eighteen-year-olds in the area, he was in love with the belle of Ross County—Alvira. To his joy she returned his love, even though suitors came from counties around to woo her. After two years, he had saved enough to marry. The wedding date was set, the wedding clothes stitched. Then, just a week before the wedding, Alvira and Enos went to the church picnic.

A stranger from a nearby village was there: Brown, he said his name was. He wore a fancy vest, a watch chain dangling with fobs, and an elegant set of sidewhiskers to match his silky mustache. The young man held Alvira's hand just a trifle longer than was necessary when he was introduced. He claimed the seat next to her, and by the time the pies were brought out, he was showing Alvira his chiming watch. Enos sat in a jealous, lump-throated silence as Brown fascinated the woman he loved.

By the time the picnic was over, Brown had Alvira's hand tucked under his arm. And he drove her home in his elegant carriage behind a pair of glossy black, high-stepping horses. Enos gazed after the cloud of dust that followed them. He heard Alvira squeal as the carriage hit a bump.

Two nights came and went, and the third morning the whole village was abuzz: young Brown had put a ladder up to Alvira's window and eloped with her behind those two glossy horses! All tongues were quick to condemn her—except Enos who was still too much in love to bandy her name about.

The last person to see him alive heard him mutter, "I'll haunt fool lovers 'till the Judgment Day...." And Enos Kay went and shot himself, out in the open, where he wouldn't give anybody any trouble to clean up after him.

Late the next day, Enos Kay was laid to rest. It was whispered that Alvira and young Brown drove slowly past the cemetery as the coffin was being lowered.

That very night at Timmon's Bridge, a nearby courting spot, two young lovers in a buggy had stopped their horse on the bridge, its top up and its curtains down. Scarcely had the couple begun to canoodle, when the buggy top was jerked down around them. They saw their horse quivering with fear—and a wispy cloud just above the buggy with a familiar face in it—the face of Enos Kay grinning madly at them. The young driver just had time to grab the reins before his spooked horse dashed down the road.

That was only the beginning. Rain or shine, dark or daylight, young lovers would find their buggy tops pulled down to expose their courting to the world. But it was only happy lovers that the ghost bothered. If a couple were quarreling, they were left strictly alone, as were single folk. To this day, Enos Kay has kept his promise to "haunt fool lovers 'till the Judgment Day."

THE RAIN DRUM

In the extreme northwestern corner of Williams County sits Nettle Lake. Sam Coon, an old trapper who lived on its banks in the 1870s, was as wild-looking as his name. He wore his hair and beard long and shaggy and matted and if he ever washed them, it was only because he'd accidentally got caught in a downpour. His clothes and shoes were pieced together out of sacking and half-cured animal pelts. On a hot day he smelled like road kill.

Coon was a spiritualist—that is, he thought he could talk with the dead and they could talk back. He kept a big Indian drum in his cabin. The few people who got close enough to look, whispered that the drum was made of human skin stretched over a bone frame, and that *something* rustled inside.

Sam Coon never would say where he had gotten the drum. He believed that a quick, angry beat on the drum summoned the spirits of dead Indian chiefs who muttered to him of treasures buried along the banks of Nettle Lake. A slower beat would call down rain, with its answering thunder.

Coon listened carefully to those Indian voices he heard telling of buried gold. He would stand in the green-slimed shallows of the lake and dig huge caves in its banks. Sometimes he would prod with an iron bar down among the cattails, the stink of marsh gas bubbling around him.

The marshes surrounding the lake were not the healthiest place to dig for treasure. One day Coon was bit by a fever-bearing mosquito. For days he burned, then he shook with ague as if something had him by the ankles. He finally died, raving of claws and scales.

Somehow his only surviving nephew heard of his death and came—supposedly to pay his respects—but really to search the cabin for the treasure the old man was said to have discovered. The nephew found nothing but the drum—with its head burst outwards, as if something that had long lain coiled within had escaped. The nephew left in a hurry, leaving what was left of the drum in the cabin. Something might want it back, he thought.

Nobody else dared visit Sam Coon's cabin and it finally fell to pieces. But on humid summer days by

Nettle Lake, when the air lies in wait for a cloud-burst, you can still hear the far-away beat of Sam Coon's drum, like the growl of a distant dragon.

THE ACCIDENTAL APPARITION

This happened in the late 1930s when not many people had autos. You'd gather a lot of people together and drive to parties or dances. This particular night, a group of teens went to a party at the Grange Hall over at Gratis in Butler County. Speeding home, they missed a curve and hit the side of the Brubaker Bridge over Sams Run Creek.

It was the middle of the night, in the middle of the open country. No one saw or heard the accident. It was only discovered by a neighbor who had come out with a lantern to check his restless livestock. He saw dark objects lying near to the bridge and found the smashed car and bodies all over his field.

He ran to his house and his wife ran to the neighbors' house for the phone. The ambulance came from the funeral home where it also served as the hearse. The farmer set up lanterns for the undertaker's men and they carted away twelve bodies.

The funeral was the talk of the county. The farmer and his wife had nightmares for months. Coming home from a Grange meeting a few nights later, their car got as far as the middle of the bridge when its lights went out and the motor died.

The farmer and his wife heard a sharp "rap rap rap"—13 raps in all—on the hood and windshield of the car. Then came a hissing sound—shhhhhh—like rushing water or wind. After only a few seconds, the lights came back on and the motor began to run again. They drove off home at top speed. Later this same thing happened to different people, and everybody began to wonder.

Then word came that a boy was missing; that there should have been another body. They'd missed his corpse the first time because his only sister said sometimes he didn't come home for days. And in the gruesome darkness of the field, nobody really knew how many bodies to look for. The searchers hunted all along the creek, but they couldn't find the body. To this day, they've never found it.

And to this day Brubaker Bridge is not a place to drive after dark. First your engine will die and then you'll hear the raps and the hissing sound. The thumpings and the hissing noises are the boy trying to get attention, to have his body found and decently buried. He drums with the stumps of his wrists because the mice have eaten away his fingers and carried the bones down their holes. And he hisses because the crows have torn out his tongue....

THE SECOND SOLDIER

At the train station, Edward Hembly's baby son played with the brass buttons on his jacket. He gave the child a kiss then handed the boy back to his wife. Edward's other son gazed wide-eyed and sucked his thumb, not quite sure about this strange man in uniform. Elizabeth Hembly's eyes filled with tears as she saw with pride how fine Edward and his older brother Samuel looked in their Union-blue uniforms.

It was 1862. The Hembly brothers were joining the 122nd Regiment of the Ohio Volunteers to fight for the Union.

The whistle of the troop train shrieked. With a last kiss for Elizabeth, Edward swung himself on board. Samuel waved and followed. The train began to move. Elizabeth ran along beside the train, calling to Samuel, "Please take care of Edward! Bring him home to us safe and sound!"

Samuel smiled, nodded, and saluted.

Edward watched his wife and sons until the train went around a bend. He was glad that the train had pulled away so quickly. The soot from the train's smokestack was making his eyes water...

The 122nd saw hard fighting and in spite of Samuel's promise, Edward was wounded and taken prisoner during the Battle of Union Mills in Winchester, Virginia on June 14, 1864. His wife Elizabeth, alone at home with their two young sons, never heard of his capture and so believed he was dead. She put on the dull black dress of a widow.

In July of 1865, Elizabeth was hanging out the family wash. Her sons were playing on the picket fence, when one boy yelled, "Ma, there are two old tramps coming down our road."

They watched as two dirty, bearded men dressed in rags shuffled slowly towards their farm. At first Elizabeth was afraid.

"You boys just go into the house," she told her sons, shooing them away from the fence. "And bolt the door."

But as the men drew nearer, she suddenly recognized the pale faces of her husband Edward and his brother Samuel underneath the dirt and rags.

Samuel stopped at the gate, then smiled and waved as his brother ran to meet his family. Edward swept Elizabeth up in his arms, and she could feel her husband's bones through his tattered uniform as he kissed her.

When she had caught her breath, Elizabeth turned, blushing, to the gate. Then she looked puzzled and asked, "Why, where's Samuel? He needs to come in and rest awhile before going on home."

Edward went pale and sagged against the fence. Elizabeth got him up onto the porch and forced some water down his throat.

He blinked up at her, then said slowly, "Samuel was killed in the Battle of Union Mills. I got off the troop train in Zanesville and walked these past five miles alone."

THE HEADLESS HORSEMAN
OF CHERRY HILL

Cherry Hill or Ghost Hill? The Fayette County hill, off Rt. 38 a mile south of Yatesville, has been called by both names. One suggests the blooming trees that covered it; the other recalls a terrible tale from long ago....

Some time in the early-nineteenth century, a man named George Oliver Smith sold his dry-goods store in Virginia and rode to Fayette County to buy a farm. Along the way he met with two men from Philadelphia who said they were patent medicine salesmen. They wore fancy vests and stickpins set with blazing jewels that they called Tibetan diamonds. And they had a hundred funny stories that kept Smith laughing until the three reached Chillicothe.

There Smith made the mistake of flashing the rolls of gold coins he carried in his saddlebags when he paid for his room. The two salesmen grew suddenly serious and said their goodbyes to Smith, claiming they needed to make some sales calls in town.

The next morning Smith rode out to Cherry Hill. He liked the look of the place and decided to stake a claim. He spent the day walking the property and making camp. That night, while he slept rolled up in his blankets, the gold-filled saddlebags under his head, the two men who had traveled with him crept up to where he lay.

Keeping well back to avoid the fountaining blood, one of them chopped off his head with the single blow of an ax. But groping around in the dark, they couldn't find the gold without getting covered in blood.

So the two culprits went back to town where they drank and got themselves thrown out of the saloon so if anybody asked, they had alibis. The next day, they went back to Cherry Hill, "looking for their friend," although they knew all along he was dead. Arriving at the spot, they found Smith's horse peacefully grazing, Smith's blanket neatly rolled up, and no trace of a body or the saddlebags!

The two men fled in terror as if the headless body was after them. They both came to bad ends.

One drowned in a horse watering trough after a drunken spree. The other died in a madhouse raving of a disembodied head dripping gold coins from the neck stump. Smith's body and head were never found.

But to this day, residents of Cherry Hill say that on clear nights you can hear the thud of the ghostly horse's hooves as he carries his headless master— forever searching for his gold, his killers, and his head.

THE RAG DOLL

Years ago, in Tuscarawas County, just as the last of the one-room school houses were dying out, the new teacher, Miss Finch, was sweeping up some bits of coal that had fallen from the scuttle. Classes had been dismissed an hour before so she was startled to see a strange little girl standing in front of her desk.

The child had dark hair sleeked into braids. She wore an old-fashioned, grey calico pinafore that was too long for her and draggled on the ground. Miss Finch looked again, raising her eyebrows. The girl's clothes were soaking wet.

The child clutched an old McGuffey reader with a scuffed red cover. She held it out to Miss Finch with a thin, trembling hand.

"Please, Miss, can you help me find my lesson?"

The little girl's voice was soft and musical. It seemed to bubble up from a long way away.

Miss Finch smiled at the child.

"Of course. Let me see your book."

It's at least twenty years out of date, thought Miss Finch, puzzled. Even stranger, the pages were damp and felt a little fuzzy as though moss were growing on them.

"This isn't our regular primer," Miss Finch told her kindly. She knew that some of the hillfolk couldn't afford new books. "But here is a lesson very like the one we're learning. Could you learn this? Then, perhaps, we can see about getting you a regular book."

The little girl nodded eagerly.

"I promise. I'll study it hard. Oh, thank you!" She turned, but seemed hesitant to go.

"Miss? I wonder—would you, could you *please* help me find my rag doll?"

"Your rag doll?" Miss Finch said in surprise. "Did you bring it to school?"

The little girl shook her head sadly.

"I only got as far as the creek...." she said. And dissolved in a kind of watery haze.

Miss Finch took off her spectacles and rubbed her eyes.

"Gracious, I must have worked too hard today!" she told herself, ignoring the small puddle of water before her desk.

And she said the same to her landlady Mrs. Douglas that evening at supper.

Mrs. Douglas put down the soup ladle so sharply she chipped the enamel.

"That wasn't no eyestrain that walked in your door," she said. "It's happened before, you know. That's why our school can't keep a regular teacher."

And she told Miss Finch the whole story.

"Many years ago when I was small, a little girl who lived nearby was on her way to school. It had rained for several days, and the creek had over-flowed its banks. The little girl tried to cross by the footbridge. She slipped and was swept away. They found her, with her schoolbook in one pocket of her pinafore. But the rag doll she always carried in the other was never found. Poor child, she's still search-ing for that doll." Mrs. Douglas shook her head.

Miss Finch went back to her room and thought a bit. Then she took out her rag bag. She sat up late that night stitching an old-fashioned rag doll with a pink calico sunbonnet and pinafore. She took out her watercolors and, by candlelight, carefully painted the doll's face with china-blue eyes and strawberry-pink cheeks.

In the morning Miss Finch slipped the doll into her pocket and carried it to school. Her mind wan-dered as her pupils recited their times tables and their spelling words. All day she wondered if the little girl would come again. But after the last student had gone, she didn't have long to wait.

Suddenly the little girl, her hair and clothing soaking wet, was standing by her desk.

"I learned my lesson, teacher," she said shyly.

Miss Finch smiled at her.

"Good for you! And I have a surprise for you. I found your doll," she said, and held it out to the little girl.

"Oh, Miss!" the little girl cried, happily pressing the doll to her cheek. "Oh, thank you!" And just as suddenly as she had come, the little girl was gone.

At supper Miss Finch told Mrs. Douglas what she had done.

"Bless you," said Mrs. Douglas, wiping her eyes. "Would you like to see her grave?"

They walked up the road to the graveyard, surrounded by a rough stone wall, the grass growing long between the grave markers.

"There," Mrs. Douglas pointed to the small stone. And she and Miss Finch both gasped. For there, lying on the little grave, was the rag doll— soaking wet.

GIRARD'S HEAD

Along the North Branch of Dick's Creek in Butler County was Girard's Point. And there, under a huge hawthorne tree, was a grave. The braver children of the neighborhood would push a big stick down into the ground with a loud thump. That thump meant that the stick was hitting the coffin of a former local schoolmaster named Girard.

Girard, a tall, slender man with a French accent, came to town in the 1830s. He had black hair and eyes and beautiful manners and would have been handsome except for one thing: he had an extremely large head. In fact, he looked like he had a pumpkin perched on his slim body. His black silk top hat, custom-made by the local milliner, was as big as a butter churn.

But Girard's personal charm was bigger than his hat size, and he managed to captivate a local girl, Miss Sally Amos. They made a pair, Miss Sally and the big-headed schoolmaster—him holding her hymnal in church, dancing a reel with her at a local ball.

"Big head, big heart!" she would say, tossing her dainty little head. Or "He's got more brains than any man in town!"

The village gossips were already setting a date for the wedding, when somebody started a rumor that Girard already had a wife and children back in France. And each time the story found a new ear, the number of children grew and grew. After a while no one knew if there really was a Madame Girard or any *infant* Girards, but the damage was done. His former sweetheart returned his letters and turned away, her nose in the air, whenever they met in the street.

Girard was so miserable, he could barely speak above a whisper in school. The children would mock him by drawing stick figures of his "wife" and twenty children on the chalkboard. As he trudged through the streets, his slender body grew skeletal.

One morning Girard's body was found dangling from the branch of a tree facing Miss Sally's house. His face was as black as the tall silk hat that lay at his feet. In it, the undertaker found a note asking that he be buried near the tree so he could watch over his sweetheart. Girard hoped to sleep there peacefully.

But a doctor arrived in the village the day after the burial, seeking permission to cut off Girard's enormous head and exhibit it as a medical curiosity. Horrified, the authorities refused.

A few days later, it was found that the grave had been disturbed. Opening the coffin, they found only the black silk hat—and a headless body.

The coffin was replaced about a foot down and from the day of the second burial, the spot was called Girard's Point. The stone marker is gone, but when you see a grinning jack-o-lantern at Halloween, cast a thought to the shallow grave at Girard's Point and that empty black silk hat.

THE BLACK DOG

In the early 1900s, it was the custom to socialize mostly with your neighbors. Most everyone worshiped at the same church and shared the same beliefs—except one young fellow named John. He was a wild one, that John—some said the worst in Putnam County.

As he grew older, he went from smoking behind the barn to drinking and sparking with the young ladies. He gambled and swore like a sailor and was heard to say that God did not exist and neither did the Devil, for if he did, why didn't Satan come and get him?

People tried to get him to hush his blasphemies, but he only cursed louder and again, laughingly called for the Devil to take him away.

One evening, right before the beginning of Lent, John went to a barn dance. As usual he drank and swore and made himself disagreeable to the ladies. He had just repeated his challenge to the Devil, when an unexpected guest arrived.

It was a large black dog, which sat at attention, waiting at the door, its eyes fixed on John. Its sleek black coat seemed to throw off little sparks of flame. The dog's ears stood up "devilishly like a pair of horns," whispered the guests. Anyone who walked by the dog caught the smell of sulphur in the creature's foul breath. The black dog's eyes seemed to glow eerily, the red-hot of smoldering coals.

Shortly before the dance ended, the dog abruptly trotted away. The dancers gave the beast worried looks as they climbed into their buggies and mounted their horses. As John rode slowly along, he swayed back and forth in the saddle, singing and swearing and calling on the Devil to come join the party.

Suddenly the black dog hurled himself out of the undergrowth. John's horse reared up, scream-ing. John fell, slamming his head into a fence post. He died instantly, his skull shattered.

The black dog didn't even stop to sniff the body, but trotted off into the night and was never seen again.

Coincidence? Or was it the Devil, so often invited, coming to claim his own?

OLD MAN PRESSOR

Old Man Pressor lived in a weather-beaten shack near Batavia in Clermont County. An eccentric loner, Pressor had cobbled together a shed over an older house's deep stone cellar and surrounded his property with "Keep Out" signs. But just as cats always climb into the laps of people who hate cats, children flocked to Pressor's shack to torment him.

Peering through a dusty window one day, the children saw him watching a beam of sunlight slide slowly across the grimy floor. When the beam reached a certain spot, the old man stuck his knife between the floorboards and lifted up a hidden trapdoor. The children ducked behind the wall as Pressor turned to face them, climbing down a ladder into the darkness. They saw a light flare as Pressor lit a candle in the basement.

It wasn't until it was nearly dark that the remaining children saw that candle, clutched in Pressor's boney hand, rise out of the trapdoor. In delighted terror they scattered to their homes with tales of Pressor, gloating in the dark over a chest of gold buried in the cellar.

The children returned day after day. Every sunny day Pressor kept his watch on the floor, then descended into the cellar. Every evening, as the sun went down, he would climb out and carefully replace the trapdoor.

The word spread about the treasure in Pressor's cellar. Pressor took to chasing the children off with an ax. He even boarded up his windows, but the children still pried at the cracks.

Pressor went to town on the first of every month. One of these days the owner of the general store was showing something unusual to a customer: a flashlight.

Pressor was immediately taken with the gadget, flicking it on and off, off and on. He bought one and enough batteries to last a year. The store owner laughed as he told people how Pressor had flickered the light all over the store.

Now when Pressor chased the children off his property, he wielded an ax—and a flashlight.

One sunny day, an adventurous little girl stayed home from school to see if she could discover what was in that cellar. To her amazement, Pressor's door was open. She stole into the house.

Dazzled by the sun outside, she couldn't see in the dark room and stumbled, falling across the open trapdoor. She heard Pressor's howl of rage and was blinded by the stab of his flashlight beam in her eyes. Frantically she scrambled to her feet, pushing over the ladder that led to the cellar. Behind her she heard a scream and a crash. Then silence.

She didn't wait to see if Pressor would follow, but ran home as fast as she could. She was too terrified to go back to the old man's shack, but other children did—and saw only the trapdoor, standing open, a dark hole in the floor.

After a few days, the girl confessed what she'd done to her father. He and one of the neighbors went to the house and found the old man lying at the foot of the ladder with a broken neck. In one hand he clutched the flashlight, in the other, he had the ax in a death-grip.

They buried him in a nearby graveyard. Not long after the funeral, a light could be seen, late at night, floating through the graveyard or bobbing over the countryside. Pressor's flashlight, say the adults, shining to show him the way out of his grave. Old man Pressor himself, say the children, shivering, searching for the girl who caused his death.

THE WORLD'S SHORTEST GHOST STORY

A man sat reading his newspaper on the bus.
The woman next to him, turned to him and said,
"Do you believe in ghosts?"
"Ghosts?" he snorted. "Of course not! Do you?"
"Oh yes," said the woman.
And disappeared.

SOME GHOSTLY (AND GHASTLY) FOLKLORE

Always hold your breath as you pass a cemetery.
Students have told me that it is impolite to breathe
when the dead can't. People used to believe that a
ghost could steal a person's soul as they breathed.

Hold up your feet as you drive by a cemetery.
Never walk on a grave.
So the spirits can't drag you down into their grave by
your feet!

The last person to be buried in a graveyard will
haunt that place until the next burial.
Two funerals on the same day often led to fights
about who would be buried first. Relatives didn't
want their loved one to be the last buried, for the
ghost would have to sit and watch the graveyard.

Ghosts can be seen in mirrors.
Mirrors have always been associated with magic.
There are many stories of people seeing ghosts
behind them in a mirror that vanish when they turn
around.

If you look in a mirror in a darkened room and say,
"Bloody Mary, Bloody Mary" (or "Mary Worth, Mary
Worth") a number of times, (usually 100), she will
come out of the mirror and grab you.

Students always ask me if Bloody Mary is real. Several have told me that they actually *saw* something coming out of the mirror at them. Let's think about this logically: you're in a dark room with several nervous friends, you've stared at yourself in the mirror or spun around a couple of times. It's dark; you're dizzy and disoriented. Sure you'll scare yourself into seeing *something*!

Ghosts can be seen if you look through a ring.

Animals, especially cats, can see ghosts better than people.
I'm often told of normally well-behaved dogs who suddenly snarl and bark when they are taken to a haunted room. Some will even refuse to enter haunted houses. If your animal suddenly starts acting like there is a threat in the room, it is possible she is really seeing something. Still, when I see a cat staring hard at something invisible, I suspect that cat is just trying to drive us humans crazy.

A cold spot means a ghost.
Of course, it can also mean a drafty window or leaky roof.

Ghosts and other supernatural beings cannot cross running water.
Remember the headless horseman who chased Ichabod Crane? He had to stop just at the edge of the bridge because he couldn't cross the stream.

Someone will die if:
A bird taps on a window
A woodpecker knocks on a house
A dog howls at night
A picture or mirror falls off the wall

A clock often stops just as a person dies.
I'm also told stories of stopped clocks that restart
themselves and chime on the date of a death. For
example, in the Harding home in Marion, a clock,
usually stopped all year, is supposed to spin to the
right time and chime the hour of President Harding's
death.

*If you shiver, that means someone just walked on the
place you will be buried.*
In England they say, "A goose just walked on my
grave." This is where we get the term "goose-
bumps."

*There are iron fences around old cemeteries to keep
the dead in and the living out.*
In the old days, iron was believed to be magical.
Ghosts could not pass iron or running water. A
more practical explanation for the fences is that in
the 19th century, bodies were often dug up and
stolen from cemeteries to be sold to medical schools.
Iron fences made it harder to rob graves. In some
early cemeteries, graves were piled with heavy
weights or stones to keep animals—and grave robbers—from digging up bodies.

HISTORICAL NOTES
AND
GLOSSARY OF
OLD-FASHIONED WORDS

p. 2 "...the curtains had been drawn, as for a funeral." When someone died, it was the custom to put a wreath on the door and draw all the curtains and window shades in a house.

p. 9 Battle of the Wilderness, fought near Fredericksburg, VI, especially at Spotsylvania Courthouse and Cold Harbor, May-June 1864. At least 60,000 Union soldiers died.

p. 19 "saved enough to marry..." In the 19th century, couples often didn't marry until the young man had enough cash to buy a house or farm.

p. 20 "a nearby courting spot, two young lovers in a buggy...." Since there were no automobiles, couples who were "courting" or dating, often drove out to the countryside in a buggy. They sometimes parked on covered bridges for privacy. The word "lover" was used for any person dating another.

p. 23 Spiritualist: A person who believes they can communicate with the dead. Holding seances was a popular entertainment in the 19th century.

p. 24 "fever-bearing mosquito...ague" Pioneers often suffered from fever and chills (or ague) after they were bitten by mosquitos carrying malaria and other diseases.

p. 27 Grange Hall: The National Grange of the Patrons of Husbandry was a club founded in 1867 so that farmers and their wives, often living on lonely farms, could get together to enjoy parties and classes.

p. 32 "dull black dress of a widow." At this time, widows were required to wear dull black clothing for the first year and a day after their husbands' deaths. For the next six months, they could wear shiny black cloth like silk or taffeta. In the next six months, they could wear "half-mourning" or whites, greys, and lilacs. Only after two full years could widows wear real colors again.

p. 35 patent medicine: A medicine usually made from "secret ingredients" plus a lot of alcohol. Many "Doctors" and "Professors" traveled around the country selling these medicines during "medicine shows" with music, entertainment, and wild claims about the miraculous powers of the patent medicine.

p. 36 "stake a claim..." To ask for legal rights to a piece of land. There was plenty of land in frontier Ohio. To get the land, settlers had to build a place to live and send in a paper filing a "claim," or claiming the property.

p. 39 One-room schoolhouse: Pioneer schools were held in one-room buildings. Grades 1-8 or 1-12 all worked together in the same room.
McGuffey reader: The McGuffey Eclectic Readers, 1836-57, were first compiled by William Holmes McGuffey of Cincinnati. The books were filled with stories, poems, and pictures and were often the only school book a child had.

p. 41 Rag bag: When clothing was too worn to mend, women cut off the useful pieces and kept them in a rag bag to be used in mending other items.
China-blue eyes: Early china often had designs printed on it in blue.
Times tables: Students recited their multiplication tables out loud in the classroom.

p. 47 Medical curiosity: Doctors often stole the dead bodies of people who had died from a rare disease or had some kind of deformity. They would dissect them and, in some cases, publically display the body or bones.

p. 54 Flashlight: The flashlight was an unusual device before the 1920s.

GLOSSARY

Bandy [a name]: Casually gossip about a person

Barn Dance: A pioneer social event where people gathered at a barn or hall for dancing and fun

Belle: A popular girl

Bogle: A creepy creature. Like the "boogy man"

Butter Churn: A tall tub where cream was churned/stirred into butter

Calico: A cotton fabric, usually dyed blue, pink, red, or grey with a black or white print

Canoodle: To kiss and hug

Cavalry: Soldiers who rode and fought on horseback

Coal scuttle: A metal box with a handle for carrying coal from the coal cellar to the stove

Fob: A fancy charm hung on the chain of a pocket watch

Hankered [for]: Wanted very much, longed-for

Hearse: A vehicle that carries the coffins of the dead

Milliner:	A hat-maker
Parlor:	A living room
Pinafore:	A dress-like apron
Pined [for]:	Wanted very much
Poke bonnet:	A cloth hat like a sunbonnet, but with a stiffer frill around the face
Saloon:	A bar
Shroud:	A cloth the dead were wrapped in for burial
Sidewhiskers:	Sideburns
Spark:	To court a young lady. To date
Stickpin:	A fancy pin worn on a man's tie
Suitors:	Men wanting to marry or date a woman
Tramps:	Men who roamed the country by foot or train, often begging for handouts or offering to do chores in exchange for food
Undertaker:	A person who prepares the dead for burial
Watering trough:	A long narrow tub for animals to drink from
Woo:	To try to attract a girl. To court

ABOUT THE STORIES

The Bride at the Bridge

Nanette Young, of Harmony Farms Stables just outside of Beaver Creek State Park in Columbiana County, told me this story. Nanette is a wonderful storyteller and she used to take people on moonlight horseback rides where she would tell this story and other local spooky tales. Nanette told me about a time she and some other riders encountered something eerie on the Beaver Creek bridge. You can read the full story in *Haunted Ohio II*.

The Seven Dachshunds

In the 1940s, a local man named Harold Igo collected and retold a number of ghost stories from the town of Yellow Springs, Greene County.

Nobody, even the town historian or librarians, seems to know anything about who Harold Igo was or why he was interested in ghosts. Some thirty of his stories were printed in the local newspaper. They are now available in the Antiochiana Room of the library at Antioch University.

The Headless Soldier

This is another story from the Harold Igo Collection. (See "The Seven Dachshunds.")

Poke-Bonnet Kate

This is part of a series of folk and ghost tales collected in the 1950s and 60s as part of a series called the "Ohio Valley Folk Publications." Various researchers collected several hundred stories and oral histories, particularly in the Ross County/ Chillicothe area. Many of these can be found at the Ross County Historical Society, the Ohio Historical Society in Columbus, and the Columbus Public Library. The ones I have seen were typed, duplicated on a mimeograph machine, and stapled together with old wallpaper samples for covers. They are crumbling to bits and I hope that someone will decide to publish all of them or take some steps to preserve them before they disappear forever.

The full title of this story is "Poke-Bonnet Kate, A folk yarn from Ross County, Ohio," Melly Scott, Ohio Valley Folk Research Project, The Ross County Historical Society, Chillicothe, OH 1961, 8th folk publication in 1961, Ohio Valley Folk Publications—New Series, No. 68

The Buggy Bogle

This is part of a series of folk and ghost tales collected in the 1950s and 60s as part of a series called the Ohio Folklore Project. (See "Poke-Bonnet Kate.")

This particular story is titled "The Ghost of Enos Kay," and was written by "Erasmus Foster Darby"—a pen name for folklore collector Dave Webb of Ross County (1904-1963). It was printed in Chillicothe in 1953.

The Rain Drum

This story comes from an old history of Williams County. My friend Linda Marcas, who lives in Wood County, found a copy of this book at a garage sale. The "book" was copied on a mimeograph machine in purple ink and stapled together. I don't know if any other copies exist.

The Accidental Apparition

Mrs. Sigie Mingie, who is a storyteller and, as she says, "resident white witch," in Germantown, Montgomery County, sent this story to me along with several others that I used in the *Haunted Ohio* series. She says that she can see ghosts and talk to them and she has one in her house.

The Second Soldier

I first saw this story in the Piqua newspaper at Halloween. Readers had been invited to send in their stories and Mrs. P. W. sent in this traditional family story. (Mrs. P. W.: Please contact me!)

The Headless Horseman of Cherry Hill

Carol Carey, director of the Fayette County Historical Society at Washington Court House, sent me this story which comes from a Fayette County history. It also was published as part of the Ohio Folklore Project (see "Poke-Bonnet Kate" notes) as "The Ghost of Cherry Hill," James E. Leasure, Jr., 1953. When I recently visited Washington C.H. I found that a school has been built on Cherry Hill.

The Rag Doll

At the Ohio Folklife Festival in Quaker City, Tuscarawas County, little old-fashioned rag dolls are sold with a version of this story attached. This story also appears in *Hants and Hangings: Stories of the Odd, the Bizarre, the Sensational in Area Early History and Folklore* by F.A. Morgan.

Girard's Head

Mr. George Crout sent me this story when he heard I was looking for tales for my *Haunted Ohio* books. It comes from the tiny town of Blue Ball in Butler County.

The Black Dog

This story was sent to me by "Mrs. B"—she asked not to be identified—from Putnam County. She heard this tale from her father—a German Catholic immigrant—who, she said, "wasn't in the habit of making things up." Sometimes she thought that the story actually happened in Putnam County. Other times, she believed that it happened to her father's father in Germany. Either way, she "never doubted the truth of the story."

Old Man Pressor

I first read this in the *Ohio Folklore Society Journal*, Fall 1968, p. 189, where it was contributed by Terri Haverkamp of Batavia in Clermont County. I have not been able to find anything more about Terri Haverkamp.

WHERE TO FIND MORE
SPOOKY STORIES

First, ask your librarian. He or she will know what books your library has and can show you how to find them. If your library doesn't have the books on this list, ask if they can order them from another library.

If you want to find spooky stories in the newspaper, look at papers from the week before Halloween, especially the Saturday or Sunday before. That is when many newspapers print local ghost stories.

Another good way is to ask your grandparents and parents and other relatives what spooky stories they heard growing up. Get a tape recorder and tape their stories or write them down. They are part of history!

AUDIOTAPES

Brown, Roberta Simpson, *The Scariest Stories Ever*, 1991

The Folktellers, *Chillers*

Gere, Jeff, *Oahu Spookies*, 1994

Graveyard Tales: Stories told at the National Storytelling Festival

Levitt, Marc Joel, *Tales of an October Moon, Haunting Stories from New England*, 1992

Martin, Rafe, *Ghostly Tales of Japan*, 1989

Reneaux, J.J., *Cajun Ghost Stories* 1992

San Souci, Robert D., *More Short and Shivery, Thirty Terrifying Tales,* 1995

—*Short and Shivery, Thirty Chilling Tales,* 1995

Torrence, Jackie, *Spooky Stories*

Richard Alan Young and Judy Dockery Young, *Ozark Ghost Stories,* 1992

—*There's No Such Thing as Ghosts, Ghost Stories from the Southeast,* 1993

BIBLIOGRAPHY

This list includes "true" stories and folktales.

Barry, Sheila Anne, *World's Most Spine-Tingling "True" Ghost Stories,* New York: Sterling Publ., 1992

Beckett, John, *World's Weirdest "True" Ghost Stories,* New York: Sterling Publ., 1992

Bodie, Idella, *Ghost Tales for Retelling,* Orangeburg, SC: Sandlapper, 1994

Brown, Roberta Simpson, *Queen of the Cold-Blooded Tales,* Little Rock, AR: August House, 1993

—*The Walking Trees,* Little Rock, AR: August House, 1991

Bullock, Alice, *Monumental Ghosts*, Santa Fe, NM: Sunstone, 1987

Cohen, Daniel, *Ghostly Tales of Love and Revenge*, New York: G.P. Putnam's Sons, 1992

—*The Ghost of Elvis and Other Celebrity Spirits*, New York: G.P. Putnam's Sons, 1994

—*Ghosts of the Deep*, New York: G.P. Putnam's Sons, 1993

—*Great Ghosts*, New York: Scholastic, 1990

—*Phantom Animals*, New York: Minstrel, 1991

—*Phone Call from a Ghost: Strange Tales from Modern America*, New York: Minstrel, 1990

—*Railway Ghosts and Highway Horrors*, New York: Scholastic, 1991

—*Real Ghosts*, New York: Minstrel, 1977

—*The World's Most Famous Ghosts*, New York: Minstrel, 1978

—*Young Ghosts*, New York: Cobblehill, 1994

Colby, C.B., *World's Best "True" Ghost Stories*, New York: Sterling Publ., 1992

Crites, Susan, *Confederate Ghosts*, Martinsburg, WV: Butternut, 1992

—*Ghosts of Christmas Past*, Martinsburg, WV: Butternut, 1995

—*More Civil War Ghosts*, Martinsburg, WV: Butternut, 1995

—*Union Ghosts*, Martinsburg, WV: Butternut, 1993

Freeman, E.M., *Campfire Chillers*, Old Saybrook, CT: Globe Pequot, 1994

Haskins, James, *The Headless Haunt and Other African-American Ghost Stories*, New York: Harper Collins, 1994

Hausman, Gerald, *Duppy Talk, West Indian Tales of Mystery and Magic*, New York: Simon & Schuster, 1994

Hayes, Joe, *La Llorona, The Weeping Woman*, El Paso, TX: Cinco Puntos, 1987

Hodges, Margaret, *Hauntings: Ghosts and Ghouls from around the World*, Boston, MA: Little, Brown, & Co., 1991

Jones, Louis C., *Spooks of the Valley*, New York: Houghton-Mifflin, 1948

—*Things That Go Bump in the Night*, New York: Hill and Wang, 1959

Kendall, Carol F., *Haunting Tales from Japan*, Lawrence, KS: Spencer Museum of Art, 1985

Knight, David C., *Best True Ghost Stories of the 20th Century*, New York: Simon & Schuster, 1984

Leach, Maria, *The Thing at the Foot of the Bed and Other Scary Stories*, Cleveland and New York: World Publishing Co., 1959

—*Whistle in the Graveyard: Folktales to Chill Your Bones*, Maria Leach, New York: Puffin, 1974

Lyons, Mary E., *Raw Head and Bloody Bones, African-American Tales of the Supernatural*, NY: Charles Scribner's Sons, 1991

Macklin, John, *World's Most Bone-Chilling "True" Ghost Stories*, New York: Sterling Publ., 1993

—*World's Strangest "True" Ghost Stories*, New York: Sterling Publ., 1991

McKissack, Patricia C., *The Dark-Thirty: Southern Tales of the Supernatural*, New York: Alfred A. Knopf, 1992

Montell, William Lynwood, *Kentucky Ghosts, Lexington, KY*: University Press of Kentucky, 1994

Rau, Margaret, *World's Scariest "True" Ghost Stories*, New York: Sterling Publ., 1994

Reneaux, J.J., *Haunted Bayou and Other Cajun Ghost Stories*, Little Rock, AR: August House, 1994

Rizzo, Rebecca, *Campfire Thrillers*, Old Saybrook, CT: Globe Pequot, 1994

Roberts, Nancy, *America's Most Haunted Places*, Orangeburg, SC: Sandlapper, 1987

—*Animal Ghost Stories*, Little Rock, AR: August House, 1995

San Souci, Robert D., *More Short and Shivery, Thirty Terrifying Tales*, New York: Delacourte Press, 1994

—*Short and Shivery, Thirty Chilling Tales*, New York: Doubleday, 1987

Schwartz, Alvin, *Ghosts: Ghostly Tales from Folklore, An I Can Read Book*, New York: Harper Trophy, 1991

—*In a Dark, Dark Room and Other Scary Stories*, New York: Scholastic, 1984

—*More Scary Stories to Tell in the Dark*, New York: Harper Collins, 1984

—*Scary Stories to Tell in the Dark*, New York: J.B. Lippincott, 1981

—*Scary Stories 3: More Tales to Chill Your Bones*, Harper Collins, 1991

Spariosu, Mihai I. and Benedek, Dezso, *Ghosts, Vampires, and Werewolves, Eerie Tales from Transylvania, New York*: Orchard Books, 1994

Viviano, Christy L., *Haunted Louisiana*, Metairie, LA: Tree House Books, 1992

One place you can find ghost story books and tapes is the catalog, *Invisible Ink: Books on Ghosts & Hauntings.*® This catalog lists over 350 spooky titles you can order. See p. 85 for how to order your free copy.

INDEX

The End

ABOUT THE AUTHOR

Chris Woodyard, shown here as Davy Crockett, age two, started seeing ghosts when she was very small. She grew up in Columbus, went to school to become a librarian, ran an antique clothing store, and wrote children's textbooks. She has also written *Haunted Ohio: Ghostly Tales from the Buckeye State, Haunted Ohio II,* and *Haunted Ohio III.* She lives in an *unhaunted* house in Beavercreek, Ohio with her husband and daughter.

ABOUT THE ILLUSTRATOR

Jessica Wiesel is a student at the Columbus College of Art and Design. She lives in a small apartment with a snake, a ferret, and a stinky cheese man.

HOW TO ORDER YOUR OWN
AUTOGRAPHED COPIES OF *SPOOKY OHIO*
AND THE *HAUNTED OHIO* SERIES
(also T-Shirts, etc.)

Call **1-800-31-GHOST (314-4678)** with your VISA or MasterCard order or send this order form to: **Kestrel Publications, 1811 Stonewood Dr., Beavercreek, OH 45432 • (513) 426-5110**

☐ FREE CATALOG! "INVISIBLE INK: Books on Ghosts and Hauntings" - Over 300 books of ghost stories from around the world!

_____ copies of *SPOOKY OHIO* @ $8.95 each $_____

_____ copies of *HAUNTED OHIO* @ $10.95 each $_____

_____ copies of *HAUNTED OHIO II* @ $10.95 each $_____

_____ copies of *HAUNTED OHIO III* @ $10.95 each $_____

_____ *Spooky Ohio* T-shirt @ $12.00 each $_____
Size ____M ____L ____XL ____XXL

_____ *Haunted Ohio* T-shirt @ $12.00 each $_____
Size ____M ____L ____XL ____XXL

+ $2.50 Book Rate shipping, handling and tax for the first item, $1.00 postage for each additional item. Call (513) 426-5110 for speedier mail options. $_____

           TOTAL $_____

NOTE: We usually ship the same or next day. Please allow three weeks before you panic. If a book *has* to be somewhere by a certain date, let us know so we can try to get it there on time.

MAIL TO (Please print clearly and include your phone number)

_____

_____

_____

_____

FREE AUTOGRAPH!

If you would like your copies autographed, please print the name or names to be inscribed. _____

_____

PUBLISHER NOSINESS: Where did you get this copy? _____

_____

PAYMENT MADE BY:

☐ Check   ☐ MasterCard   ☐ VISA

($15 min. order on credit cards)

Card No. _____   Expiration Date:

Signature _____   Mo_____ Yr_____